The "Old White Hotel"

THE GREENBRIER

A Great American Tradition
Since 1778

Contents

Springhouse Levee at the temple of Hygeia, White Sulphur, 1870

THE GREENBRIER

A Great American Tradition

A word of history and assurance to all of our Guests: to those of the recent past, and may they return again and again; to those of the present, now possibly experiencing The Greenbrier for the first time; and to the many others who may read this and be influenced to come to "White Sulphur."

PERHAPS no resort in the United States is richer in historical, political and cultural tradition than The Greenbrier at White Sulphur Springs in the Allegheny Mountains of West Virginia. Its existence virtually spans the national existence of our country, for it was in 1778 that the first of many generations sought the benefits of White Sulphur's restful waters, the exhilaration of its superb climate and the wonderful serenity of its lofty hills and shaded valleys.

Shortly after the close of the 18th Century, White Sulphur gained stature when rows of cottages were built on the slopes immediately surrounding the Springs — Alabama, Louisiana, Paradise, South Carolina and Baltimore Rows which today still adorn the grounds of The Greenbrier.

The first hotel was quick to appear on what is now the site of the Lester Building and soon White Sulphur Springs became the social "Summer Home" of the entire East . . . as the Clays, the Jeffersons, the Carrolls, the Popes and others of the "First Families" flocked here with their outriders and slaves. Prominent journalists of the time variously described it as The Grand Emporium of Fashion, or The Paradise of Enjoyment.

As a booming by-product of its success, White Sulphur Springs became the nation's leading Marriage Mart. In fact, the necessity for organization became the mother of the invention of the renowned Billing, Wooing and Cooing Society. Launched in 1832, the Society was no figment of idle whimsy. On the contrary, it represented a very business-like affair, complete as it was with a Constitution, Code of

A Great American Tradition

Idyll on a Cottage Verandah
from Harper's Weekly, 1888

Rules and Ethics and a membership list of no less than 1,700 names . . . each of which was finely inscribed on a magnificent pink scroll that hung on the walls of the Grand Ballroom for all to observe.

By 1850, such was the popularity of White Sulphur that princes and potentates and the great and the near-great of that period flocked to it. Old registers show that Presidents Van Buren, Tyler and Fillmore made it their Summer White House and that nine other Presidents have been our guests. Finally, demand for accommodations so greatly exceeded supply that plans for a great and wondrous new hotel were drawn up, and, in 1858, scores of workmen applied the finishing touches to a gleaming edifice which was to become beloved and famous throughout the world as "The White."

No sooner did it open than "The White" became filled to capacity with notables, world-travelers and the Grand Belles, those glamorous debutantes of their time who added a scintillating aura to the setting. Among the famous first guests was the Prince of Wales of bon vivant fame who later became King Edward VII of England.

Soon, however, the ominous shadow of the "War Between the States" lengthened up this peaceful valley and across the lands beyond. From 1861 to 1865, "The White" was occupied as a hospital at various times by Confederate or Union troops as the lot of the struggle swung from one side to the other.

With the end of the Civil War, the revival of The Springs was slow. However, when General Robert E. Lee chose to make his summer home here in Baltimore "G" Cottage for the years 1867-68-69, the old glamour and standing returned.

"All times are attractive at this historic old place, the one golden link yet remaining between the past and the present," wrote Aubin McDowell fifty years ago, "still embodying the gay, brilliant life and generous hospitality, typical of the Old South, added to its great natural advantages for the physical well-being as well as the enjoyment of mankind."

The vast estate changed hands again when the Chesapeake & Ohio Railway purchased it in 1910. Improvements of the grounds, restoration of the building, and plans for a new hotel . . . all began immediately. And in 1913, The Greenbrier, a magnificent Georgian structure of some 250 rooms, was completed to take its place among the social centers of this continent and Europe very quickly.

In 1930-31, the original Greenbrier was virtually rebuilt . . . with the North Wing and the Virginia Wing added to the reconstructed center section, increasing the capacity of

The Greenbrier to 600 rooms. At the same time the building that houses the beautiful mosaic pool and the Baths, was joined to the North Wing—then certain cottages were restored, and sports facilities developed and modernized.

The Greenbrier weathered the depression to a new peak of success when, in 1941, it became a "conscript" of World War II, first serving as an internment center for enemy diplomats and later as a General Hospital.

At the war's end, the property was re-acquired from the Government by the Chesapeake & Ohio, and the U. S. Army "moved out" in that expression's fullest sense—lock, stock and barrel. A titanic task of redecoration faced the talented Dorothy Draper who was assigned the job of recapturing the glories that had been The Greenbrier's. It is said that never before in the history of interior decoration has a restoration at so high an aesthetic level or on so huge a scale been attempted, and so successfully accomplished.

With infinite imagination, daring creative ability and fine taste, Mrs. Draper and her staff developed literally over a thousand variations of the strikingly beautiful dominant color scheme. In upholstery, floor coverings and draperies, in bedspreads and in the famous pink and green dining-room china, the Draper designs were carried out by master craftsmen.

The impact of The Greenbrier decor has no doubt been an influence in thousands of American homes and studios.

Another point in this complete project of restoration was the design and coordination of the gardens and landscape surrounding The Greenbrier. This included the development of the forecourt, the wall garden, fountains and terraces, to say nothing of the selection of garden and terrace furniture, and even to lilies on the steps and tulips at the fountains. Seen now through the bay windows of the Old White Club, these details make a most enchanting picture, difficult to forget.

As a final note, perhaps one of the most exquisitely beautiful touches by Dorothy Draper is the re-creation of the old-fashioned Grand Ballroom. This, more than any other aspect of The Greenbrier, symbolizes the spirit and majesty of its venerable past, when White Sulphur was referred to as "The Athens and Paris of America" and guests of "The White" enjoyed a life that, on reflection, must have been indeed "only slightly removed from heaven." Here, on a gay evening of your own, you'll see the magnificent crystal chandelier gleam like a great jewel as its sparkling reflections illumine the soft pink walls, the draped satin curtains and the gilt dancing-school chairs, for there's dancing here

every evening except Sundays, during Spring, Summer and Fall.

That one of West Virginia's former governors, William Alexander McCorkle, found that his *History of White Sulphur Springs* called for a volume of over 400 pages, that in Perceval Reniers' lively and readable book, **The Springs of Virginia,* largely devoted to White Sulphur, the Bibliography alone exceeds four pages, will explain why the long, exciting and significant history of this famed resort can only be hinted at here. Two things impress the student, first, that for over 150 years writers have been quite carried away with the charm, the beauties, the fascination of White Sulphur, and second, that each generation has voiced a fear that the changes wrought here by war and reconstruction would impair or destroy something that was so dear to them.

But back in 1878 *Harper's Magazine* reported "in the midst of the fast and somewhat pretentious and shoddy existence of the present time, you find here the same air of high-breeding and rational relaxation which characterized the White Sulphur during the *ancien regime."*

A generation or so later Charles Dudley Warner was to write "For the better part of a century the White Sulphur has been, as everybody knows, the typical Southern resort, the rendezvous of all that is most characteristic of the South, the meeting place of its politicians, the haunt of its belles, the arena of gayety, intrigue and fashion. In the days of its greatest fame it was at once the finest and most aristocratic assembly in the world . . . "

You who are now at The Greenbrier for the first time must see that a sincere attempt has been made to surround our guests with beauty and every possible comfort, to anticipate your every wish and need, also that there is a quick, courteous, experienced response whenever special service is required. But you came here, probably, expecting to be pleased; while the former guest of twenty years ago, with fond memories of near-perfection, on his return to The Greenbrier today is quite prepared to be disappointed with what the 1950's have done to his beloved resort. How welcome then is a comment such as the one we shall now share with you.

A Californian who had been a year-after-year "regular" through the 1930's, but whose 1954 visit was the first in fourteen years, had many things to tell us. Let us quote his warm approval:

> " . . . almost every change has been for the better. The Greenbrier is lovelier and finer than ever . . . a most magnificent restoration . . . it seems the impossible has been accomplished . . . even the food is better, the service superb.
>
> "The new wing . . . is a long step in the right direction . . . the removal of meetings from the public rooms . . . the restoration of the matchless Virginia Room to the enjoyment of guests . . . all most desirable.
>
> "For all its grandeur and beauty, the true appeal of The Greenbrier lies in its background and history of culture and gracious living . . . a great hotel it is, probably the most magnificent in this country, or any other, but beyond and above all that, it is a national shrine, just as truly as are Mt. Vernon and Monticello.
>
> "Those things I have mentioned, the President's Cottage, the cottage where General Robert E. Lee lived the summers of 1867-68-69, the famous old Carolina, Georgia, Alabama "Rows", the murals, prints and

*University of North Carolina Press, 1941.

original paintings, are, as at Mt. Vernon, or The Hermitage, or the State House at Philadelphia, but symbols of time and events. . . . They tell us of the great national figures, of the thousands of notable men and women who visited here . . . of plans of vital national importance formulated here . . . especially during the reconstruction era . . . they tell of chivalry and romance too, of stately ceremony and sparkling gayety. . . .

"The Greenbrier has no equal and no rival. There is nothing like it and it is certain that there never will be anything like it again."

Yes, it seems as though some magic ink has touched the pens of our admirers with living fire, so that the glow of their honest admiration often flames into ecstasy. What a responsibility is ours then, we who are charged with carrying on the great tradition! We do not, we cannot, promise perfection, but we aim for it, and in the satisfaction of our guests . . . such satisfaction as expressed by President Dwight D. Eisenhower after his meeting here in 1956 with President Adolfo R. Cortines of Mexico and Prime Minister Louis St. Laurent of Canada . . . we find our greatest reward.

The Greenbrier is so much more than a hotel or the smartest and gayest of resorts. It is a yardstick by which to measure our country's growth. Considered as an entity, it represents and reflects the cultural and traditional attainments of our nation's lifetime. It is thoroughly American . . . in its character, in its charm and in its dedication to our earliest and highest concepts of hospitality and service. The Greenbrier of today is indeed A Great American Tradition.

YOUR ROOM AT THE GREENBRIER

has been decorated by Dorothy Draper with fully as much care and attention as she would accord a room of her own, considering first of all your comfort and, next, the creation of an atmosphere of complete charm. The furnishings are of the fine quality you prefer in your own home. If this is your first visit to The Greenbrier, you'll be interested in these features of your home-away-from-home:

Because even in mid-summer the evenings may be brisk and breezy, we first direct your attention to the heat-regulating thermostat on the wall. Just set the indicator at the desired temperature.

Your door will automatically snap-lock on closing, so, when you leave your room, be sure to take your key. If absolute privacy is desired, use your key to lock the door from the inside. No other key can then open it.

If you do not wish to be disturbed by the maid making her daily check of your room or by bellmen, messengers and others, please hang the "Do Not Disturb" card outside your door. For complete privacy, follow these steps: (1) hang out the sign, (2) use the key to lock your door from the inside and (3) ask the telephone operator to hold all calls until further notice.

If you wish to have your room made up and in order by a certain hour, mark the time on the card provided in your room for that purpose and place it on the outer door handle.

For additional linens, towels or blankets,

ask your maid. If the maid is off duty, call the Linen Room. If needed, the Linen Room will also be glad to supply, at a moderate rate, ice packs, hot water bottles, electric pads, cotton blankets, health boards for your bed and bed extensions for tall persons.

Throughout your quarters you will find adequate electrical outlets—AC ONLY—110 Volts. Should you desire an iron or ironing board, these are available through the Linen Room without charge.

A safe is provided at the Cashier's desk for the deposit and safekeeping of all money, jewels and other valuable articles. Unless so deposited, the Management cannot be liable for the loss thereof.

LAUNDRY

A modern laundry, offering quick and efficient service, is operated by The Greenbrier. Laundry received by the Bell Captain by 10:00 A.M., will be returned about 5:00 P.M., the same day, if requested. Any clothing received after that time will be returned the following day at 5:00 P.M. Unless special service is required, only one delivery is made each day.

Laundry bags will be found in the clothes closet of your room and the laundry list is in the writing desk. A place is provided on the list for any special instructions you may wish to give the laundry . . . such as information regarding starching garments.

If you would like to leave your soiled clothes with us upon departure, we will be glad to finish them and mail your clean laundry to you postage paid. Please write your name and address on the slip for this purpose found in the desk and we will take care of the rest.

VALET

Near the north entrance on the Shop floor is a completely equipped Valet Shop, open daily from 7:00 A.M. to 8:00 P.M. In addition to dry cleaning and pressing, expert repair service is available in an emergency. Special attention is given to ladies' gowns and garments.

Your clothing can be dry cleaned, pressed and returned by 6:00 P.M. the same day provided it is picked up before 10 o'clock in the morning . . . please phone the Valet Service and a messenger will promptly pick-up and deliver your garments.

GARAGE AND LIMOUSINE SERVICE

Open 24 hours every day of the year, The Greenbrier's fireproof garage has individual automobile stalls, many steam-heated for winter use. Motor fuel is available and the garage also has facilities for lubrication, oil change, washing, waxing, simonizing and minor repair work. For prompt delivery of your car, call Limousine Service.

Limousine Service also provides 24-hour transportation for guests who did not bring their own automobile. Limousines are available, too, for sightseeing tours at varying rates depending upon distance and waiting time involved. Greenbrier Limousines meet all trains.

Bus transportation between the hotel and the Golf and Tennis Club and the Swimming Club is provided free of charge. The bus leaves from the Main Entrance of the hotel at 15-minute intervals. Should you prefer a Limousine for this short trip, the charge is nominal.

Also available is a U-Drive-It-Service if you would enjoy driving to the many nearby points of interest. Call U-Drive-It-Service or inquire at the Limousine Office at the front door of the hotel.

DOW-JONES SERVICE PUBLIC STENOGRAPHER NOTARY PUBLIC

The latest, up-to-the-minute market information from Dow-Jones is listed near the Western Union Office on the Registration Lobby Floor. The Public Stenographer has a desk in the Resident Manager's Office on this same floor. If you wish secretarial work done on Saturday afternoon or on Sunday, please make arrangements in advance. The Assistant Manager on duty will call a Notary Public when necessary.

HIGHWAY AND AIR TRAVEL

The Public Stenographer has highway information, maps, travel literature, and she can offer you complete AAA service. She also has a current Airlines Guide and will be happy to take care of your reservations on Greenbrier Charter Planes and on scheduled airlines.

DRESS AT THE GREENBRIER

Life at The Greenbrier is happy, friendly . . . comfortable, and we dress accordingly. There are few restrictions on dress at The Greenbrier. We've observed most guests are governed as to dress by the spirit, the setting and the season. As to the spirit, The Greenbrier is informal by day; gay and carefree by night. As to the setting, shorts and slacks may be worn at the sports areas – the Swimming Club and the Golf and Tennis Club–and on the lower lobby floor, but they are not seen in the main dining room, main lobbies or at tea. Gentlemen may wear sports shirts, closed at the neck, with a jacket, in the main dining room at breakfast and luncheon. A tie is required at night. Guests may sunbathe on the terrace adjacent to the indoor pool and at the Swimming Club, but brief attire is not permitted on the hotel's West Terrace. Riding clothes may be worn at breakfast and luncheon.

As to the season, country attire is prevalent for daytime wear with sweaters, tweeds and top coats necessary in Spring and Fall. Guests at The Greenbrier often dress for dinner: simple gowns or cocktail dresses for ladies, black tie for gentlemen. In the Winter, guests generally dress for dinner on Friday and Saturday nights only. Sunday night is traditionally an informal night, all year around.

DINING AT THE GREENBRIER

Our three main dining salons—The Colonnades, The Georgian Room and The Terrace Room—are located at the south end of the Main Lobby Floor. The beautiful Mural Dining Room is at the entrance to the West Wing. All dining rooms are air conditioned. Dinner music is a nightly feature.

During Spring, Summer and Fall, a hot and cold buffet luncheon is served each day at the Golf and Tennis Club. Gentlemen will also enjoy the informal atmosphere of the Men's Grill at the Club.

All of these Dining Rooms operate on the American Plan and your meals are included in the daily tariff. If you desire a particular waiter or waitress for a given occasion or a regular table assignment for your entire visit, please advise the Headwaiter, for The Greenbrier abides by the union request of rotating waiters and waitresses to different tables at each meal.

Then, too, you may wish the luxury, pleasure and comfort of a leisurely, sumptuous meal served by Room Service in the privacy of your own room at a nominal service charge. Room Service is also available at the Cottages.

Food service hours are listed in the Directory of Hotel Services. *Should you wish to miss the crowd, when a large cocktail party is scheduled it is best to plan to dine before 8:00 p.m.*

STATE LIQUOR AGENCY

West Virginia law permits the open sale of alcoholic liquor only at State-controlled liquor agencies. The State agency at The Greenbrier is located in the hotel near the North Entrance on the Registration Lobby level. Here guests may purchase their requirements from a full and complete stock at State-controlled prices.

Hotel bellmen and waiters are permitted, with a guest-signed order, to make these purchases for delivery to guest rooms or to the Old White Club in the member's name. Wines and Beer may be purchased in the dining rooms.

OLD WHITE CLUB

The air-conditioned Old White Club, The Greenbrier's popular cocktail lounge and after-dinner rendezvous, is located near the dining rooms. *Under West Virginia law, membership in the Club is obligatory for the use of its facilities.*

Guests may procure their membership cards in the Club. Each member is then assigned a locker where his beverage supplies are kept. These beverages remain the member's property and will be served only to him. Set-ups are provided at moderate cost. A member is charged a nominal fee for each non-member guest.

The Old White Club is open daily from noon until midnight, with dancing before and after dinner.

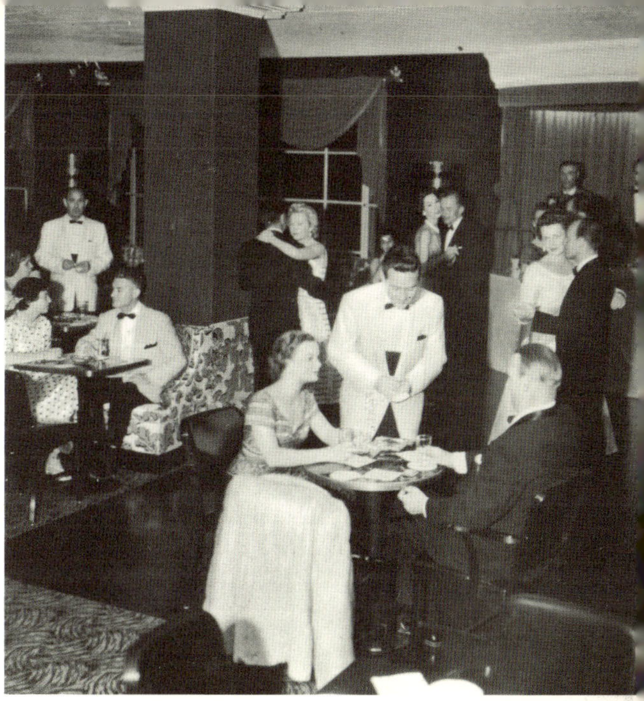

SOCIAL ACTIVITIES

To note the daily social activities which have earned for The Greenbrier its reputation as America's Smartest and Gayest Resort, please consult the bulletin board located near the main dining rooms. Here you will find posted the current social events and sports programs, theatre features, the daily weather report and other topics of interest.

Should you wish any particulars of the social program, our Social Director, whose office is on the Registration Lobby Floor, will welcome your queries.

Tours, conducted for those interested in decorating and the history of the resort or the plantings and gardens of The Greenbrier estate, are scheduled regularly by the Social Director and the Resident Naturalist.

CHILDREN'S PROGRAM

The Greenbrier is a happy playland for children . . . particularly during the summer months when a supervised play program is in effect for youngsters from 3 through 14 years of age. Please ask the Sports Director for details.

Baby-Sitting Service, both during daytime and evening hours, is available through the Housekeeping Department.

Special children's parties may be arranged through the Dining Room Captain. Given advance notice of your child's birthday, we will be happy to provide a beautifully decorated cake at a reasonable cost.

THE COTTAGES

The Greenbrier's historic cottages, several of which have been in continuous use for more than a century, offer you the informal charm of your own home . . . plus all the advantages of hotel service. The larger cottages have full-size kitchens, so you may "eat in" or you may enjoy all your meals in the hotel, as you prefer. The Rates . . . both European and American Plans . . . are available from the Reservation Manager on request. The cozy sitting room-bedroom combinations of Georgia Row, one of the oldest cottage rows at The Greenbrier, which has been recently restored, have individual verandas. The Greenbrier's cottages are very popular with families, small congenial groups and honeymooners, too.

THE GOLF AND TENNIS CLUB

Favorite daytime rendezvous of both sportsman and spectator is The Greenbrier's Golf and Tennis Club, just a short walk from the North Entrance or a quick bus trip from the Main Entrance.

Surrounding the homey, plantation-like club is one of the country's finest golf layouts . . . two championship eighteen hole courses, the Old White and the Greenbrier, the tricky little nine-hole Lakeside links and a driving range . . . five fast Har-Tru tennis courts, a practice putting green and excellent facilities for shuffleboard, horseshoes, croquet, and archery. Nearby is the Swimming Club with its large, free-form outdoor pool, sun-bathing terrace and snack bar.

During Spring, Summer and Fall, a hot and cold buffet luncheon is served each day from Noon until 3 p.m. at the Golf and Tennis Club. The Men's Grill, a male bailiwick, which is also open each day for luncheon, is on the lower floor of the clubhouse, off the men's locker room.

GOLF AT THE GREENBRIER

Golf and The Greenbrier have been synonymous for a good many generations, for it was back in 1884 that a group of transplanted Scotsmen first brought the game to our picturesque valley. Historians have said that Oakhurst, located not far from today's Old White Course, was the first organized golf club in the United States. It was not long before the patrons of the famous Old White Hotel, who at first had been amused at the sight of grown men chasing a small guttapercha ball, became addicts of the game of golf.

Today, in what the late revered golf journalist, O. B. Keeler, described as "the most beautiful inland setting of any golf courses in America," The Greenbrier offers you two championship 18-hole courses, the Old White and the Greenbrier, and the challenging 9-hole Lakeside Course.

The Old White Course was originally laid out in 1914 by Charles B. MacDonald, one of the finest golf architects of all time, and it has tested the games of such famous golfers as Bobby Jones, Walter Hagen, Lawson Little and Helen Hicks. The Greenbrier Course, also designed by MacDonald & Raynor was added in 1926. Although no date is available for the construction of the Lakeside Course, there is evidence it was in use long before the Old White Course was built.

In our constant effort to make these three courses among the finest in America, we have recently improved the locations of tees and traps.

Your clubs will be given complimentary transportation to the Golf and Tennis Club office. If you do not accompany them, your clubs will await you on the rack in front of the downstairs Golf Desk.

Tee priority may be arranged with the Starter at the Number One Tee of each course.

The Golf Shop carries a complete range of equipment. Each day, on arrival at the Golf and Tennis Club, please register with the Golf Manager if you intend to play.

If you will then advise the Caddy Master of your proposed starting time, he will take your clubs from your locker and assign them to a caddy.

TENNIS

Five fast Har-Tru courts provide ideal conditions for tennis fans to enjoy a fine game. Located in front of the Golf and Tennis Club, the courts have been the scene of many stirring matches.

The nation's top-seeded players have long participated in tournaments sponsored by The Greenbrier for the pleasure of its guests. Among the former winners of these historic tournaments are some of the truly great names in tennis . . . William T. Tilden, Jr., Francis X. Shields, Ellsworth Vines. Special exhibitions and informal tournaments for guests are also held from time to time. A favorite spectator sport, tennis is also an exciting diversion for those relaxing on the clubhouse veranda.

Instruction is available for beginners or those who wish to increase their skill. Rackets may be rented and supplies are available at the tennis Pro-Shop at the courts. Locker and shower facilities are located on the lower floor of the Golf and Tennis Club.

RIDING AND DRIVING

Horseback riding and driving are two of the most popular sports at The Greenbrier where a stable of excellent horses is maintained throughout the year.

Winding through the woods of the lovely Alleghenies and around the golf courses, twisting through country alluring in its rugged beauty and challenging in adventure, are more than two hundred miles of well-kept trails.

You may follow a stream on horseback through the cool forest, pause on top of a windswept knoll and watch the panorama of Greenbrier Valley stretch out in shifting patterns of light and shade. Or, if you wish to relax in a comfortable vehicle behind a pair of smart-stepping horses tooled by a competent coachman, you may enjoy the scenic beauty with ease from the seat of a carriage or buckboard.

Riding lessons under the direction of competent instructors are available. Guides familiar with the various trails and the lore of the countryside are on hand to accompany you.

The Mounting Ring and the office of the Riding Master are at the North Entrance.

THE GREENBRIER RIDING TRAILS

	Miles
FOREST DRIVE	6
VALLEY VIEW	7
CATAMOUNT	7
HUNTERS	5
KIRKLAND	5
NICELY	2
FREELAND	5
KATE'S MOUNTAIN	10
O'CONNER	2½
GREENBRIER	14

Trail Maps Available at Livery Office

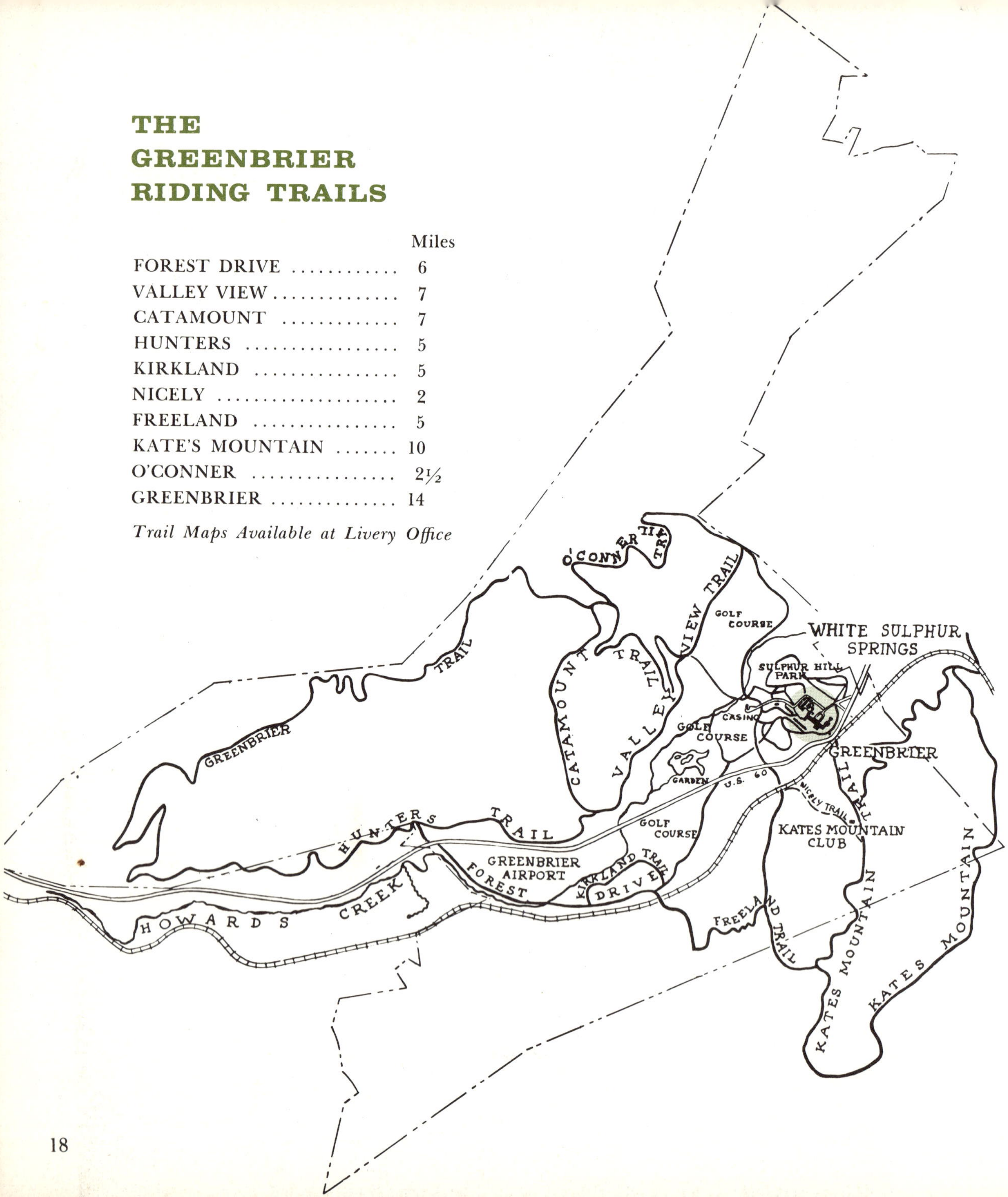

SWIMMING

Superb swimming is a year round feature at The Greenbrier.

Located near the Golf and Tennis Club, the new Swimming Club was designed to complement the scenic mountain view. Open from early Spring to late Fall, its free form outdoor pool is rectangular at the diving end and perfectly round at the shallow end. This was done so that in effect, the pool is two pools . . . those who prefer swimming can do so in the circle, which has a diameter of 80 feet, without interference from the divers. The pool is 135 feet long and holds 350,000 gallons of water. The continuous flow of filtered spring water is kept at a perfect swimming temperature through an automatic thermostatically controlled heating system. There is a complete change of water every 8 hours. The Swimming Club has a Snack Bar and a canopied dining area for those who prefer a light luncheon at the poolside. It also has a wide, beautifully landscaped terrace for sun-bathing. A wading pool is the children's delight. The Club's daily charge includes the use of all facilities . . . locker, towels, and lounge. Weekly and monthly rates are also available.

In the Bath Building near the North Entrance on the Registration Lobby level, is one of America's largest indoor pools. Built of Mosaic tile and also continuously fed by the Alvon Spring, the pool is kept at a constant temperature of 77 degrees. The indoor pool is open whenever the outdoor pool is closed, providing guests with all-weather swimming.

Many colorful water ballets and diving exhibitions are held throughout the year at both pools.

Pool hours are from 10:00 A.M. until 6:00 P.M. Expert instruction in swimming and diving is available at reasonable rates.

THE GREENBRIER GUN CLUB

Located at a particularly scenic site on Kate's Mountain, the Club has four combination trap and skeet ranges for shooting. From these four fields and from the clubhouse veranda one has a commanding view of the grandeur of West Virginia's Alleghenies to the north and east.

Just a five minute drive from the Main Entrance, the Club has ample parking facilities, or you may take one of our Greenbrier limousines to the field.

Expert instruction is available. A large assortment of guns and jackets are on hand for those who did not bring shooting equipment.

Open the year round, the Greenbrier Gun Club has been called one of the outstanding shooting layouts in the country. Please call the Club Manager for additional information or for an appointment.

FISHING

The streams of Greenbrier County are ideal for trout, pike and bass fishing during open season. Howard's Creek, which winds through The Greenbrier's golf courses, is well-stocked with brook, brown and rainbow trout.

Flowing within five miles of the hotel, is the Greenbrier River with its magnificent, untouched river scenery. Mountains rise from its banks as high as 1,000 feet in places, and along its course there are excellent opportunities for photographing the beautiful scenery and wildlife.

Both the Greenbrier River and nearby Anthony's Creek are bass streams. Swan Lake, on the hotel estate, provides all-season fishing.

A non-resident fishing license is necessary. The Assistant Manager on duty will give you full information.

OTHER SPORTS

Those who prefer less strenuous sports may find archery, putting, horseshoes or shuffleboard to their liking. Facilities for these sports are on the lawns adjacent to the Golf and Tennis Club. There is also a new 18-hole putting green on the West Lawn of the hotel. These minor sports add to the enjoyment of life at The Greenbrier. They are available throughout the Spring, Summer and Fall, and there is no charge.

CYCLING

The Walking Trails around The Greenbrier's estate are perfect for mile after mile of easy cycling, providing exhilarating exercise amid scenic beauty. Bicycles, including tandems, may be rented by the day at the Riding Office at the North Entrance.

WALKING TRAILS

The Greenbrier's 6,500 acre estate strongly appeals to guests who love the great outdoors. On the hotel staff is a Resident Naturalist who conducts regularly scheduled nature tours and hikes during Spring, Summer and Fall. Numerous walking trails, ranging from short level walks to mountain climbing, have been laid out throughout the estate.

Along them, flowering shrubs and trees, as well as wildflowers, abound in Spring and Summer. Pink and white dogwood and the red blossom of the Judas tree brighten the trails. Mauve and white trillium and wild honeysuckle bloom in profusion along with West Virginia's state flower, the rhododendron. In Fall the changing colors of the foliage seem to convert the mountainsides into a giant tapestry of brilliant autumnal hues.

Heavily wooded, the Greenbrier estate is a sanctuary for birds and other wildlife. Grey squirrels, flying squirrels and rabbits, quite tame, are often seen on the lawns. Bird watching fans will note a wide variety of their feathered friends at The Greenbrier, for White Sulphur is midway between the Atlantic flyway and the Mississippi flyway and, especially during migratory season, birds from both these flyways may be spotted.

Be sure to take your camera with you on the trails for some wonderful pictures of natural scenery.

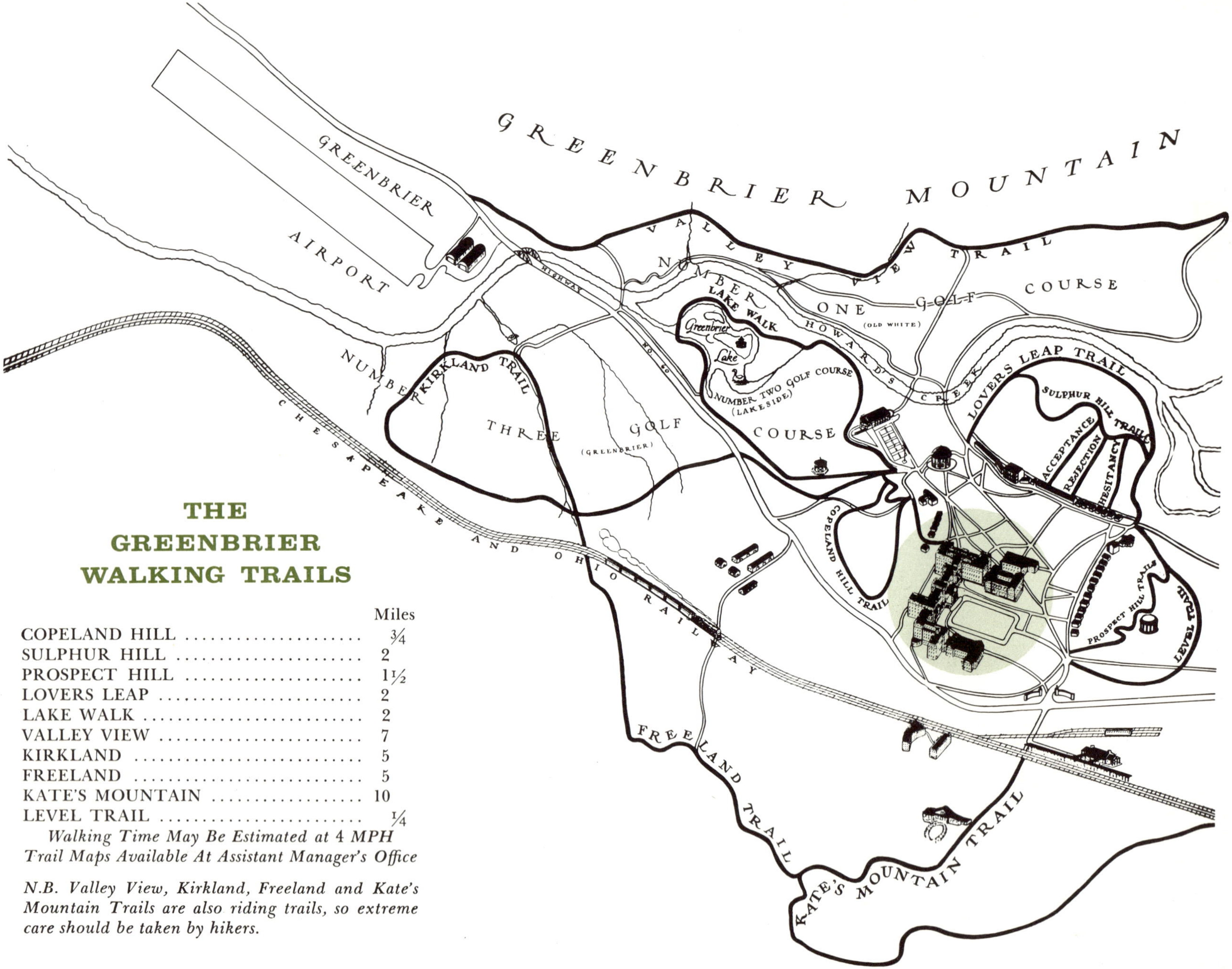

THE GREENBRIER WALKING TRAILS

	Miles
COPELAND HILL	¾
SULPHUR HILL	2
PROSPECT HILL	1½
LOVERS LEAP	2
LAKE WALK	2
VALLEY VIEW	7
KIRKLAND	5
FREELAND	5
KATE'S MOUNTAIN	10
LEVEL TRAIL	¼

Walking Time May Be Estimated at 4 MPH
Trail Maps Available At Assistant Manager's Office

N.B. Valley View, Kirkland, Freeland and Kate's Mountain Trails are also riding trails, so extreme care should be taken by hikers.

KATE'S MOUNTAIN LODGE

Another delightful facet of Greenbrier living is the rustic and charming Kate's Mountain Lodge, just five minutes drive from The Greenbrier. Artfully landscaped into the side of the Allegheny peak, named after Kate Carpenter, the handsome field-stone and timber lodge is the site of informal steak cook-outs and barbecues.

Pine-scented breezes mingle with the aroma of succulent charcoal broiled steaks and great roasts prepared in two huge fireplaces. Dance floors inside the lodge and in the open air pavilion area under the lodge's beamed roof provide a spacious setting for your evening's entertainment.

Scenic Kate's Mountain, itself, has a story to tell . . . the first owner of the White Sulphur Spring was Nathaniel Carpenter who received a land grant from George III in the early 1700's and built a log cabin near the now famous spa.

Even with a fort at nearby Lewisburg there were frequent Indian raids in the area. One day Nathaniel answered the call to aid another settlement some miles away leaving his wife, Kate, and small daughter, Frances, at home. He never returned.

Kate, herself, was forced to flee from the Indians with little Frances and went into hiding on a neighboring mountain, which has been known since as Kate's Mountain. Some men on a hunt for beaver hides found Kate and her daughter and took them to Staunton, Virginia. Although Kate was now the owner of the White Sulphur Springs property she could not bear to stay there alone.

As Frances grew into a beautiful young lady she was met and wooed by Michael Boywer. Soon after their marriage Kate Carpenter died and the White Sulphur became the property of the Boywers. A shrewd young man, Michael Boywer recognized the value of the springs and built the first log cabins to accommodate the health-seekers who arrived in larger numbers each year. From this grew The Old White and The Greenbrier.

And so The Greenbrier Gun Club and Kate's Mountain Lodge stand on the green slopes of Kate's Mountain, not far from the spot that sheltered Kate Carpenter and her small daughter.

Kate's Mountain Lodge is a part of the romantic background of the Allegheny Mountains and an evening cook-out at this convivial spot adds a special fillip to any stay at The Greenbrier.

The lodge is available for private parties. Arrangements for cocktail parties, buffets and dances may be made through the Catering or Sales Department.

THE MINERAL BATHS AT THE GREENBRIER

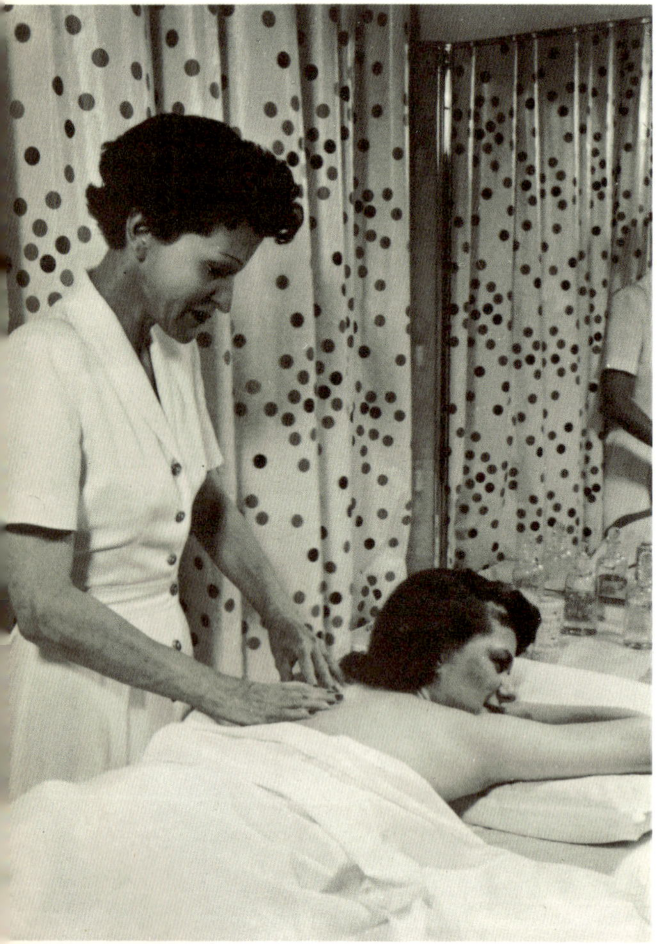

Undoubtedly one of The Greenbrier's outstanding features, the Mineral Bath Department is on the Main Lobby Floor of the Bath Wing. Countless generations have used the waters of our famed White Sulphur Springs combined with massage to ease tension, taut muscles and nerves, for The Greenbrier's mineral bath treatment is a soothing and relaxing experience.

Back in 1849 the Sears Pictorial Description of the United States stated, "Lord Morpeth and other distinguished foreigners have in their admiration pronounced the bath and White Sulphur Springs for arrangement and extent of accommodations, scenery, and health-giving qualities of the waters far superior to any similar resorts in Europe."

Down through the years claims have been made that the waters of the White Sulphur Springs have "cured" everything from alcoholism to rheumatism. The only claim we make today is: The Mineral Baths "cure" fatigue.

And once you lean back, immersed in the warm sulphur waters, you will agree. You can actually feel the fatigue gradually leave your body. Then, after the radiant pleasing heat of the electric cabinet or steam room, a series of needle, scotch and fan sprays make you exhilaratingly aware of a returned and renewed vitality. And finally, you will have the delightful relaxation of a thorough massage. This entire regimen requires approximately one hour.

Now, if you like, you may stretch out for a nap in the quiet comfort of a private room. You'll sleep, completely rested, completely refreshed and very much at peace with the world.

Although not a cure, the mineral baths may alleviate muscular pains and aches, and certain rheumatic and arthritic conditions have been known to react beneficially to mineral baths and to various other hydro-therapeutic treatments followed by Swedish massage. Other physiotherapy facilities, including diathermy machines, are available upon doctor's prescription. Whatever the treatment, skilled attendants supervise every phase of the work.

The Mineral Bath Department is open from 9:00 A.M. to 6:00 P.M. Monday through Saturday and from 9:00 A.M. to 12:00 Noon on Sundays. Please telephone the Mineral Bath Department for an appointment. Sunday appointments should be made the previous day.

THE CLINIC AT THE GREENBRIER

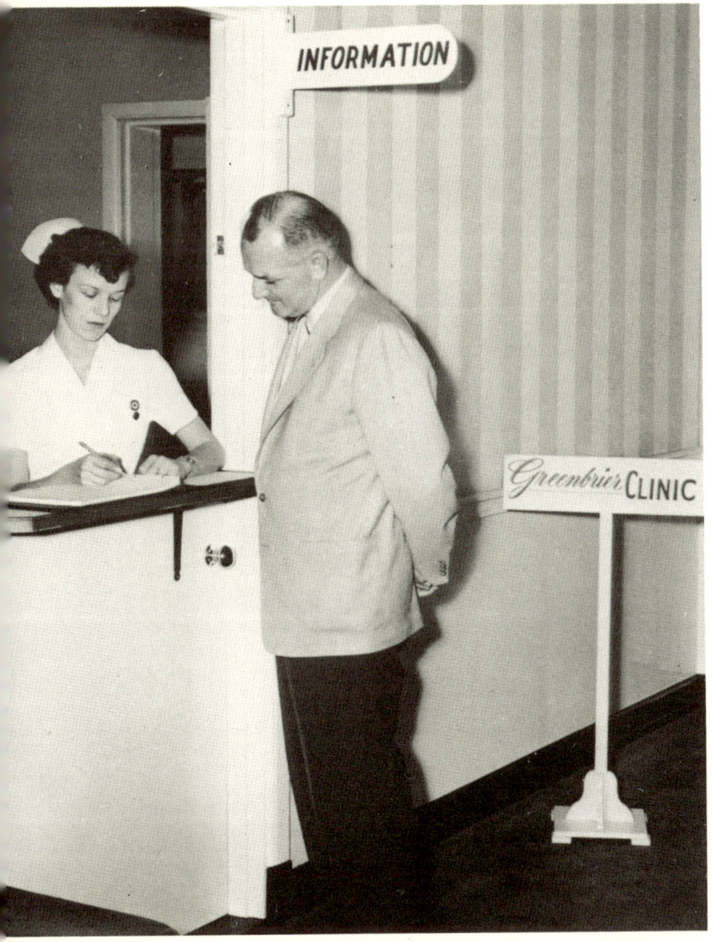

Did you know that some Orientals pay their personal physicians only when they are well? It's true! And have you ever wondered why we don't give more thought to following such a common-sense practice? We do at The Greenbrier!

The Greenbrier Clinic was planned and equipped especially for carrying out diagnostic health examinations of individuals and of groups of business and industrial executives. It is devoted to the principle of keeping you well—when you're well—rather than curing you after you've been struck down by illness. Although it occupies one floor of the Bath Wing of The Greenbrier, the Clinic is not part of or associated with the hotel operation. It is under the direct supervision of the Medical Director and is operated by him and his associates. The professional and technical staff of the Clinic works closely with a Medical Advisory Council composed of twenty-two outstanding members of the medical profession.

A complete health examination, which normally requires three days, includes reviewing your medical history and a general physical examination, fluoroscopic study of the heart, chest X-ray, electrocardiogram, blood and urine studies, as well as most special studies that are necessary for diagnosis. The only additional charges are for X-ray examinations that may be indicated.

If, during your stay at The Greenbrier, you wish detailed information about the Clinic, the Assistant Manager of the hotel will be glad to arrange an introduction to the Medical Director or a member of his staff.

ALVON SPRING WATER

Even the hot water at The Greenbrier is potable, for the hotel draws its entire water supply from Alvon Springs located twelve miles from here. Piped directly from the spring in the bedrock of the Allegheny Mountains to The Greenbrier, this water is exceptionally pure and has very little mineral content. Owned by the resort, the Alvon Springs also supplies the village of White Sulphur Springs with water.

WHEN IT'S SLEEPY TIME DOWN SOUTH

Many of our guests come to The Greenbrier for rest, as well as for the social activities and sporting events. They will appreciate your consideration in maintaining quiet on the bedroom floors after midnight. The sleep-inducing night air of the mountains also seems to reverberate sound, so we ask our guests to please speak softly when it's sleepy time down South.

TRANSPORTATION TO AND FROM THE GREENBRIER

The Greenbrier, located on the main line of the Chesapeake & Ohio Railway, with scenic U.S. Highway 60 passing its front gates and served by the Greenbrier Airport, is easily accessible to North, South, East and West.

TRAIN—All Chesapeake & Ohio trains, featuring the most modern streamlined, all-room sleeping cars, stop at White Sulphur Springs. Convenient overnight service is available from the large metropolitan cities, New York, Philadelphia, Washington, Cincinnati, Louisville, Columbus, Cleveland, Toledo and Detroit, with a few daylight hours added to the journeys from Chicago and St. Louis. Chesapeake & Ohio passenger representatives in these cities will gladly handle your reservation requests. The overnight sleeping car from New York, Philadelphia, Baltimore and Washington is set off at White Sulphur Springs in the morning and may be occupied until 8:00 A.M. The Chesapeake & Ohio ticket office, located on the Registration Lobby Floor of The Greenbrier, will be pleased to handle your return transportation.

PLANE—The Greenbrier Airport, located only one mile from the hotel, provides exceptional facilities for charter or air-taxi service to connect with scheduled airline flights in Charleston, West Virginia, Roanoke, Virginia, and other points.

With a 3,500 foot concrete runway plus a 1,500 foot sod extension, full servicing facilities, two-way radio communications and a radiobeacon, this is an outstanding field for corporate and executive aircraft of the largest types.

Ample parking facilities are available for aircraft, and direct telephone service with Roanoke Weather Bureau and Roanoke Control Tower is provided.

The air-taxi service, featuring the latest-type planes, is operated by a former major airline pilot. This service is on a reservation basis. Although there are no definitely scheduled flights, numerous trips are made each day according to the travel desires of Greenbrier guests. From The Greenbrier, via this connecting service, it is possible to reach Miami in about five hours; Chicago within four hours; and in less than three hours you can be at LaGuardia Airport in New York.

Flight arrangements can best be made direct with Greenbrier Airlines by letter, wire or telephone. It is suggested that reservations be made as far in advance as possible.

Your airline reservations may be made through the Public Stenographer in the Resident Manager's Office on the Registration Lobby Floor, or directly with Greenbrier Airlines via its hotel extension.

AUTOMOBILE—The coast-to-coast U.S. Highway 60 passes immediately in front of The Greenbrier and excellent connecting highways make driving to White Sulphur Springs an easy journey. A pleasant six-hour drive from Washington (with a few added hours for other northeastern centers) can include the beautiful Skyline Drive of the Blue Ridge Mountains, while Cincinnati and Columbus are only an approximate eight hours away, passing spectacular Hawk's Nest and other West Virginia mountain vistas. Highway maps and travel information may be secured from the Public Stenographer in the Resident Manager's Office on the Registration Lobby Floor.

CLIMATE AT THE GREENBRIER

With an average annual Mean Temperature of 53.9°, and an average of 20 sunny days a month, the climate at The Greenbrier is indeed temperate. There are many good days for golf in winter, so our courses are kept open all year round. The Greenbrier's elevation of 1,925 feet keeps summer evenings pleasantly cool even though daytime temperatures may rise to the low 80's. Spring and Fall offer perfect "suit" weather.

A temperate climate . . . glorious foliage . . . interesting mountain formations . . . an abundance of beautiful birds and other tiny wildlife . . . Mother Nature has indeed blessed our upland valley.

THE VIRGINIA ROOM

Those historians interested in The Greenbrier's colorful past will want to visit The Virginia Room, located in the Virginia Wing on the Main Lobby Floor.

Here are the famous murals, painted in the early 1930's by William C. Grauer, noted artist from Cleveland, Ohio, who directed the Art Colony here before World War II.

The panels, recently restored by Mr. Grauer, depict the story of the development of the White Sulphur Springs. Beginning with the tribes of Shawnee and Cherokee, whose hunting grounds were these wooded Alleghenies, and advancing through the coming of the locomotive and the eventual construction of the "new Greenbrier," the murals give you a vivid picture of the intriguing history of White Sulphur. Mr. Grauer did extensive research on the resort so that the costumes and life of bygone days at the Springs would be accurately reproduced.

Pioneers, stage coaches, a hunt led by Millard Fillmore, Robert E. Lee chatting with friends, the world renowned Old White Hotel . . . all are pictured in the Virginia Room murals.

There is also a television set in the Virginia Room for those who wish to keep tabs on their favorite programs.

NEARBY POINTS OF INTEREST

During your stay, or traveling to or from The Greenbrier, you may wish to visit some of the many nearby places of interest. Here are a few of the scenic and historic sights within a 100-mile radius of The Greenbrier.

Lewisburg . . . the County Seat of Greenbrier County, is a picturesque little town 9 miles west of U.S. Highway 60. Here are the Old Stone Church, the oldest church, unrestored and in continuous use, west of the Alleghenies; the Daywood Art Gallery; the Greenbrier Military School and Greenbrier College for Women.

Humpback Bridge . . . a short distance east on U.S. Highway 60—one of the few remaining covered bridges in this area.

Elmwood . . . a famous home located at Union, a small town not far from here on Route 219, South. Built in 1838, it was the scene of many brilliant social functions.

Organ Cave . . . a few miles from The Greenbrier, it was once known as "General Lee's Underground Powder Works." Organ-like white stalactite formation produces notes of varying pitch.

Droop Mountain Battlefield State Park . . . about 40 miles from here on Route 219, North. This 265 acre park embraces part of the site of the last major battle of the Civil War.

Hot Springs . . . a town of historic interest in the Warm Springs Valley of Virginia —home of the famous Homestead.

Natural Bridge . . . one of the seven wonders of the new world. It has been described as "the bridge of years" that "spans a river, bears a great highway and makes two mountains one." Once used as a shot tower, its saltpeter cave also produced powder for the War of 1812. Underground river, waterfall, trees and many scenic features may be seen.

Lexington . . . the seat of two great Southern educational institutions, the Virginia Military Institute and Washington and Lee University. Here are found the homes and tombs of General Robert E. Lee and General Thomas J. (Stonewall) Jackson. Monuments to these men and the trophy room at V.M.I. are particularly interesting.

THE PRESIDENT'S COTTAGE

Built in 1816 by Stephen Henderson, a sugar planter from New Orleans, the President's Cottage was the first of the grand "private" cottages to go up at the White Sulphur Springs. High on a bluff, the two-story pillared home created a sensation. From here the "sober sided gentleman" could survey all that went on at the Springs.

The showplace of the spa for many generations, the lovely old house became known soon after Henderson's death as the President's Cottage because many of our Chiefs of State made it their summer White House.

The first President known to have stayed at White Sulphur Springs sometime in the 1830's was Andrew Jackson. In the height of the greatest financial panic this country has ever known, Van Buren and other statesman came to White Sulphur Springs to find calm seclusion.

John Tyler is said to have spent his honeymoon in the President's Cottage. His wife, Julia Gardiner, a greaty beauty and famous Belle, created quite a sensation, for at receptions she wore three royal plumes in her hair and received her subjects seated.

Millard Fillmore, Franklin Pierce, Zachary Taylor, and James Buchanan all left their mark on The Greenbrier's Civil War period of history. After the "Peace", President Ulysses S. Grant made a visit to the Old White and was received with great courtesy along with the leaders of the South.

President Woodrow Wilson's visit at The Greenbrier in 1916 was the last appearance a President in office had made at the Springs until President Eisenhower was here in 1956 with the President of Mexico and Prime Minister of Canada for the famous three-country conference.

Mrs. Wilson, as fond of the Springs as was her husband, became a member of The Greenbrier's summer colony, returning year after year. In 1932 she dedicated the Museum in the President's Cottage which had been restored and filled with mementos of the early days at The Greenbrier.

This museum was dismantled during World War II when The Greenbrier joined the services by becoming an army hospital and the President's Cottage a Red Cross center. In 1956 the arduous task of the physical restoration of this classic building, the only example of Federal Architecture to be found in this area, and the reassembling of the colorful historical material granted to other museums and universities was begun.

The murals and panels are among the most significant of these historic items in the four room President's Cottage. They depict civil war battles, General Lee on his horse "Traveler," and days of The Greenbrier's "golden age" when silks and crinolines fluttered about on sunny lawns and gallant gentlemen played croquet and went on hunts.

CREATIVE ARTS COLONY

A new summer feature at The Greenbrier. A colony of artists is again in residence at picturesque Alabama and Louisiana Rows, the little white cottages built in the early part of the 19th century by those who came to our mountain to escape the excessive summer heat of the "low" country.

A project that was extremely popular at The Greenbrier before the war, the Arts Colony of the 1930's was a school for young hopefuls who found a wealth of beauty here.

The new Creative Arts Colony has taken a different form. Established expressly for those who vacation here, the Creative Arts Colony features demonstrations and instruction in the handicrafts which are capturing the imagination and interest of many thousands of persons all over the United States today.

WINTER-TIME AT THE GREENBRIER

The vacation season never ends at The Greenbrier — whether you are spending long, lazy summer days; crisp golfing and hunting-weather fall days; charming restful, country-winter days or sparkling, fresh spring days there are always varied activities and pleasant social occasions.

Winter is wonderful at White Sulphur Springs. The average winter temperature is about 50 degrees. There are usually 20 days of sunshine each month. The golf courses and the gun club are open all year and there are many refreshing horseback or carriage riding days.

During Christmas and immediately after the holidays there may be snowfalls which add lustre to the beauty of the countryside. When the weather outside is snowing, inside The Greenbrier fires are glowing in the great fireplaces, the glamorous Indoor Pool is temperature controlled, the cheery Terrace Room is the scene of bridge, canasta and backgammon and the tea-time concert finds guests comfortably ensconced in the Garden Room for an hour of Meyer Davis music and social conversation. Even more indoor recreation activities are scheduled for Greenbrier guests with the completion of the beautiful new West Virginia Wing.

At Christmas the pace has always been that of perfect, luxurious leisure—while the superb hotel staff plans for the guest's com-

plete enjoyment of this gayest of all holidays. A joyous Wassail Bowl, caroling, a colorful Yule Log Ceremony, Santa's visit and a sumptuous Christmas dinner have been only a part of Christmas plans.

New Year at The Greenbrier has been ushered in each year with a gala ball—a special evening of dinner and dancing in Chesapeake Hall from early evening until 2 o'clock of the New Year.

The Greenbrier is especially favored for an after-holidays breather, with a program of rest and relaxation to return you to the workaday world immeasurably refreshed and rejuvenated. Here is the time to banish tension with the soothing mineral baths and Swedish massage and to succumb to the slow pace of informal country life in the Georgian Dining Room and The Old White Club. The matchless service and efficiency of The Greenbrier staff will give you a real vacation of a few days or several weeks without a worry or a care.

An attractive "inclusive" rate is in effect during December, January, and February —the Reservation Manager will be happy to tell you about our wintertime plan.

SHOPPING ON LITTLE FIFTH AVENUE

For those moments between golf and tennis or swimming and horseback riding or for a quiet day of rexalation, The Greenbrier's lower lobby is a veritable avenue of enchantment for those of you who wish to browse, buy gifts for friends back home or do some serious shopping.

Known as "little Fifth Avenue" the shop corridor includes smart and exclusive branches of famous New York, Washington and Palm Beach shops. Ball and cocktail gowns, sports clothes for men and women, perfumes, lingerie, toys, books, records, antiques, jewelry, leather goods, linens and sweetmeats are all available in The Greenbrier's complete shopping center.

The shops are a pleasure to visit because of their attractive and individual decor and enticing displays and the superlative special attention to each customer that you do not find in metropolitan stores.

The top brands of equipment for the golfer and the tennis player are stocked in Sam Snead's Pro Shop at the Golf and Tennis Club and the Tennis Shop just off the Har-Tru courts where the sales forces are top professionals who can offer expert advice on just which equipment to select.

In addition, The Greenbriar has its own beauty shop, barber shop, railroad ticket agency, airline ticket desk, post office, telegraph office, theatre, stock exchange ticker, photography shop and laboratory, resident physicians, resident dentist, drugstore and West Virginia State Liquor Agency.

Purchases in any of the "little Fifth Avenue" shops may be charged to your Greenbrier hotel account.

YOUR DEPARTURE FROM THE GREENBRIER

These procedures will assure you of the minimum of effort and detail.

ON CHECKING OUT—Please, at your earliest convenience, advise the Front Desk of your anticipated departure time. In turn, they will notify the Cashier so that you will not have to wait for your bill. If you'd rather not pack soiled shirts, underwear, etc., fill out the address slip, send it with your clothes to our laundry and we'll mail them on to you gleaming white and sparkling clean. If you've clubs at the Golf Club, call the Golf Desk and we'll deliver them to your car, plane or train space. For the removal from your room of hand-baggage, call the Bell Captain. For the shipment of trunks or other baggage, call the Porter. Finally, if you're traveling:

BY AUTO

If your car is in the Garage, call Limousine Service and specify the time you'd like to have it delivered to the Main Entrance. To have your car in perfect order for your trip, make arrangements the night before to have it washed and fully serviced with gas and oil by expert garage attendants.

BY TRAIN

Space reservations and tickets can be obtained at the C & O Office in the Lower Lobby. Better service can be rendered on return reservations if you will give the Ticket Office ample advance notice of your anticipated departure. When your bags are packed, call the Bell Captain, giving him train time, car number and Pullman space. If you have golf clubs, give this same information to the Golf Desk. Thus you will enable us to deliver your luggage to you—on the train.

BY PLANE

Flight arrangements to all points can be made by calling the Greenbrier Airport. When your flight departure time has been determined, call Limousine Service for transportation to the Airport and call the Bell Captain who will assign a Bellboy to accompany you and handle your luggage.

On saying "Farewell," we hope your journey homeward will be a safe and pleasant one . . . and that the happy memories you take with you will aid in speeding your return to The Greenbrier.

THE NEW WEST WING OF THE GREENBRIER

The Greenbrier's new, air-conditioned West Wing was planned especially to provide today's businessman with matchless conference facilities for groups from 10 to 1,000.

Its great auditorium—Chesapeake Hall—will comfortably seat 1,000 for a meeting and 850 for a banquet. When used in conjunction with the Mural Dining Room, which opens onto one side of the Hall, the area can accommodate 1,000 for a banquet.

A theatre, seating 400 and equipped with a Cinemascope screen, is on the lower lobby floor. Both Chesapeake Hall and the theatre have a completely equipped stage, orchestra pit, and public address system. The latest 35mm and 16mm motion picture projectors are available.

The second floor of the West Wing is devoted to meeting rooms of varying sizes. These eleven rooms are ideal for committee meetings or conferences attended by 8 to 125 persons.

Our Sales Director, whose office is on the Registration Lobby Floor, will be pleased to give you information.

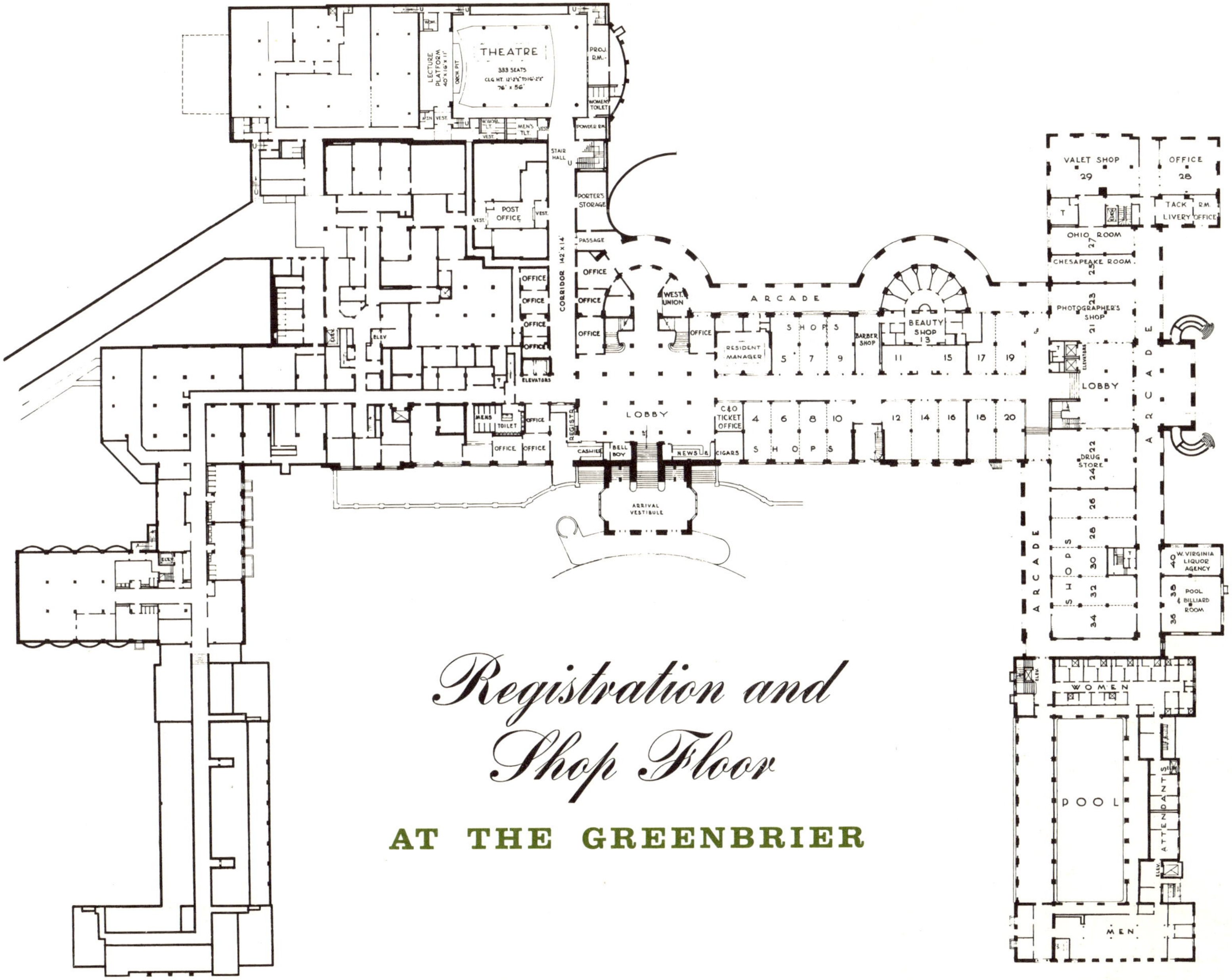

Registration and Shop Floor

AT THE GREENBRIER

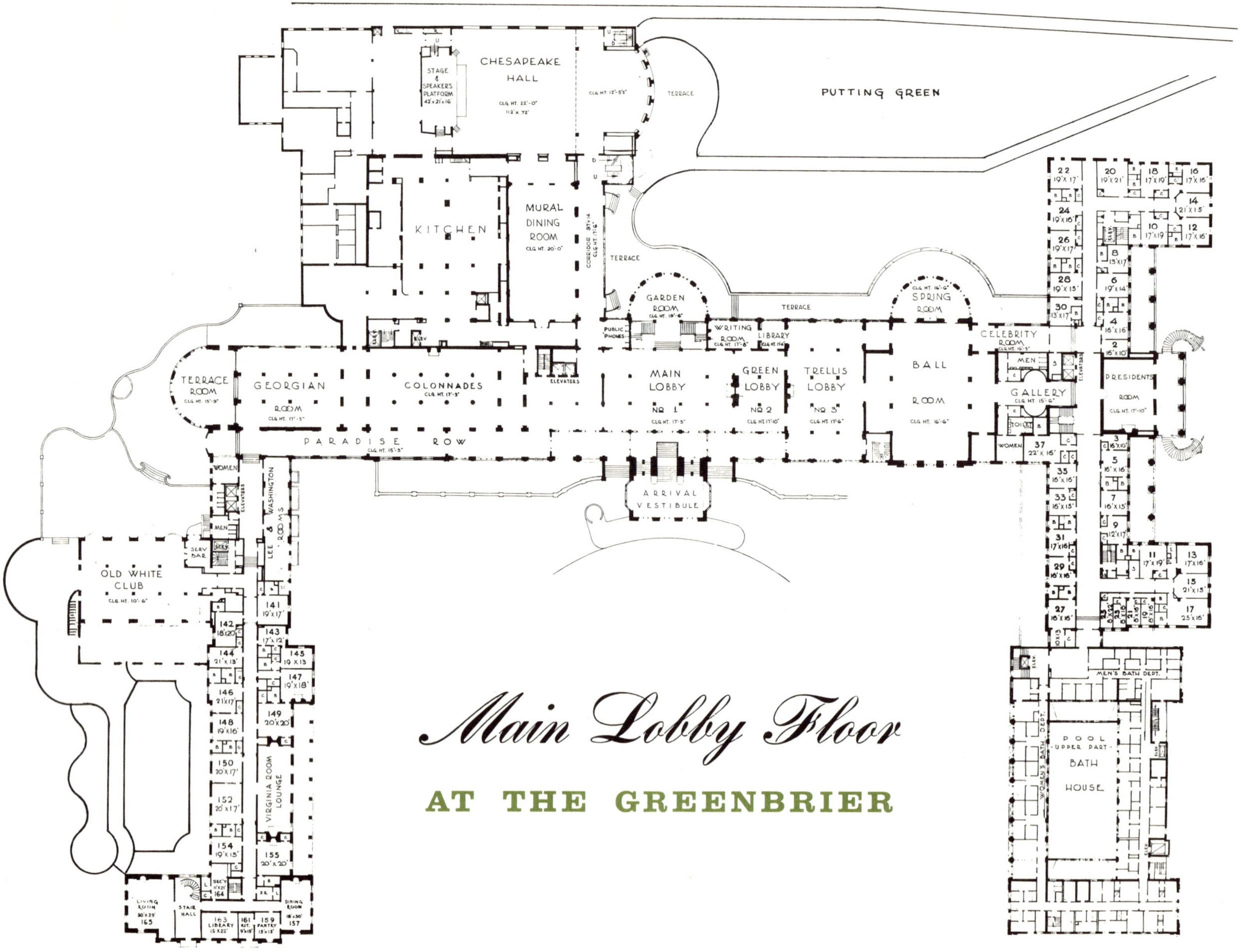

Main Lobby Floor

AT THE GREENBRIER

1961

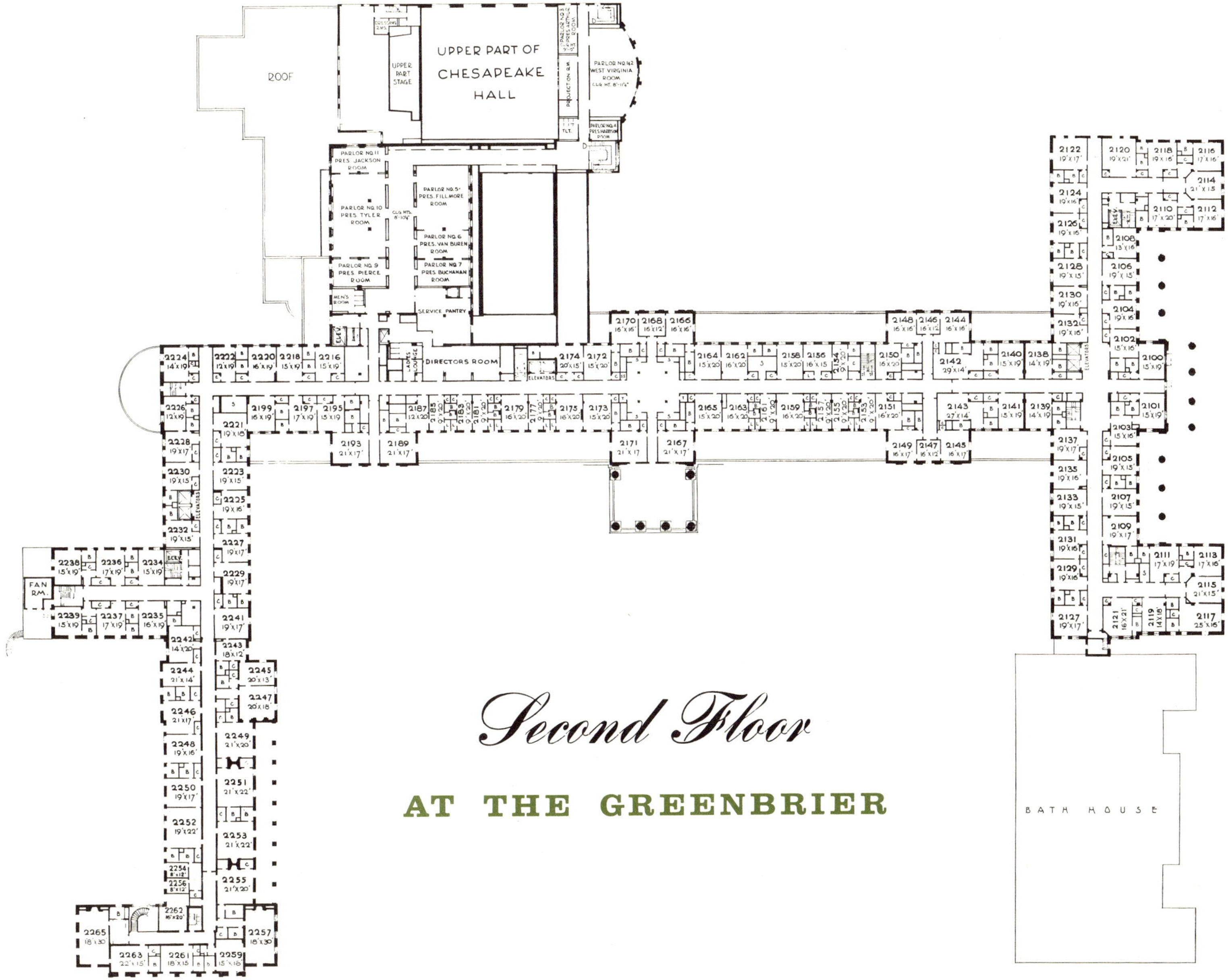

Second Floor

AT THE GREENBRIER

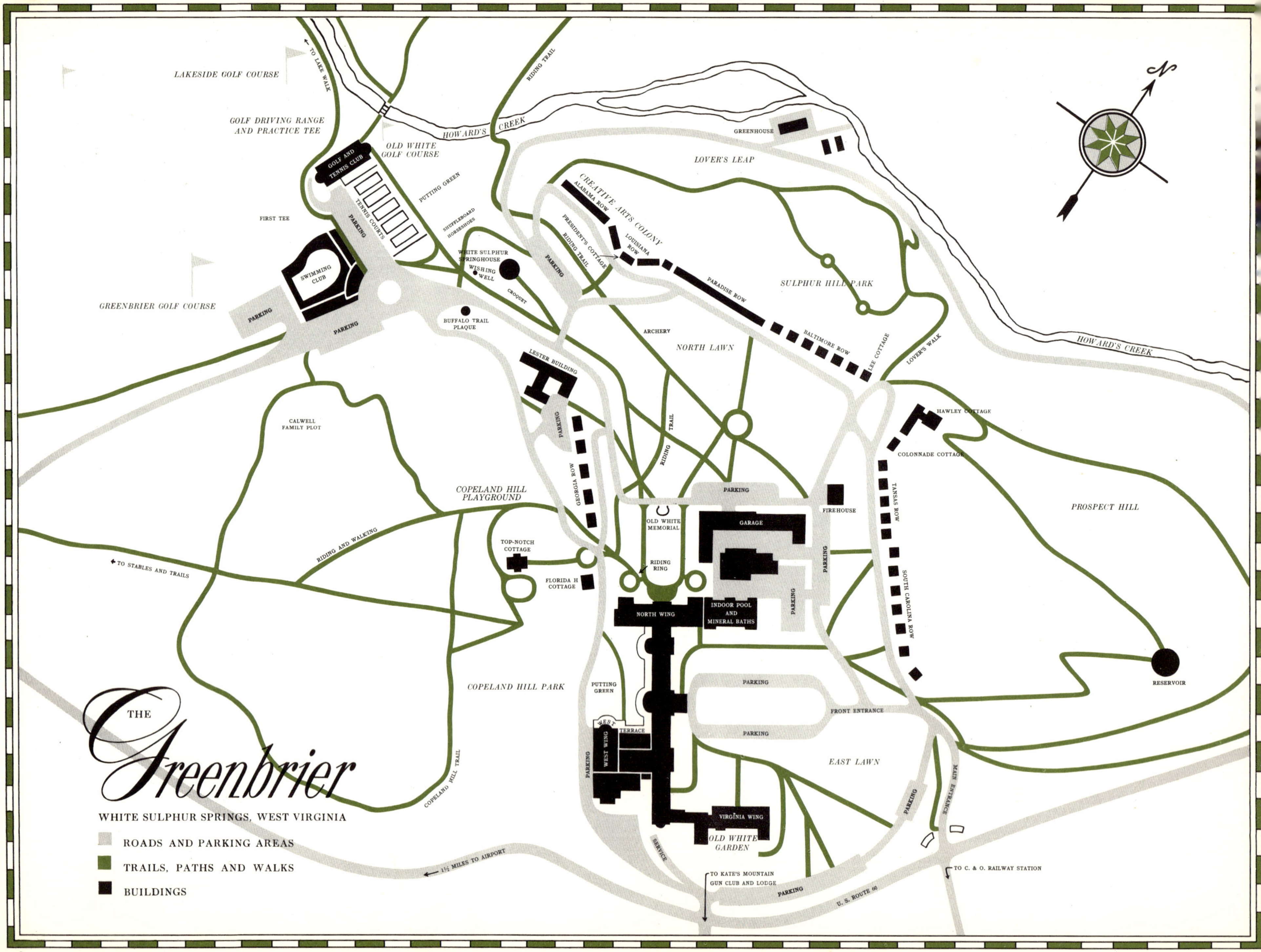
THE Greenbrier
WHITE SULPHUR SPRINGS, WEST VIRGINIA
ROADS AND PARKING AREAS
TRAILS, PATHS AND WALKS
BUILDINGS
LAKESIDE GOLF COURSE
TO LAKE WALK
GOLF DRIVING RANGE AND PRACTICE TEE
OLD WHITE GOLF COURSE
HOWARD'S CREEK
RIDING TRAIL
GOLF AND TENNIS CLUB
TENNIS COURTS
PUTTING GREEN
SHUFFLEBOARD
HORSESHOES
FIRST TEE
PARKING
SWIMMING CLUB
GREENBRIER GOLF COURSE
WHITE SULPHUR SPRINGHOUSE
WISHING WELL
CROQUET
BUFFALO TRAIL PLAQUE
GREENHOUSE
LOVER'S LEAP
CREATIVE ARTS COLONY
ALABAMA ROW
PRESIDENT'S COTTAGE
LOUISIANA ROW
PARADISE ROW
SULPHUR HILL PARK
BALTIMORE ROW
LEE COTTAGE
LOVER'S WALK
ARCHERY
NORTH LAWN
LESTER BUILDING
CALWELL FAMILY PLOT
GEORGIA ROW
HAWLEY COTTAGE
COLONNADE COTTAGE
COPELAND HILL PLAYGROUND
FIREHOUSE
GARAGE
OLD WHITE MEMORIAL
TANSAS ROW
PROSPECT HILL
RIDING AND WALKING
TOP-NOTCH COTTAGE
TO STABLES AND TRAILS
RIDING RING
FLORIDA H COTTAGE
NORTH WING
INDOOR POOL AND MINERAL BATHS
SOUTH CAROLINA ROW
RESERVOIR
COPELAND HILL PARK
PUTTING GREEN
WEST TERRACE
WEST WING
FRONT ENTRANCE
EAST LAWN
COPELAND HILL TRAIL
MAIN ENTRANCE
VIRGINIA WING
OLD WHITE GARDEN
SERVICE
1½ MILES TO AIRPORT
TO KATE'S MOUNTAIN GUN CLUB AND LODGE
TO C. & O. RAILWAY STATION
U. S. ROUTE 60